THE HAUNTED CAMPGROUND MYSTERY

GHOST TWINS

THE HAUNTED CAMPGROUND MYSTERY

Dian Curtis Regan

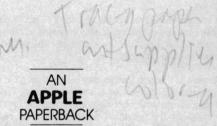

AN
APPLE
PAPERBACK

SCHOLASTIC INC.
New York Toronto London Auckland Sydney

ISBN 0-590-25242-9

Copyright © 1995 by Dian Curtis Regan.
Map copyright © 1994 by Cindy Knox.
All rights reserved. Published by Scholastic Inc.
APPLE PAPERBACKS is a registered trademark of Scholastic Inc.

12 11 10 9 8 7 6 5 4 3 2 1   5 6 7 8 9/9 0/0

Printed in the U.S.A.   40

First Scholastic printing, July 1995

For John P. Regan
and his twin sister, Mary Regan Tavolott

Contents

Tuesday, August 25, 1942   *5 cents*

JUNIPER DAILY NEWS

New Fall Fashions Inside!

Twins Involved in Boating Mishap

Robert Adam Zuffel and his twin sister, Rebeka Allison, seem to be victims of a boating accident at Kickingbird Lake. Their dog, Thatch, disappeared with them. Family members say that the twins had gone hiking on Mystery Island and were probably returning when yesterday's windstorm blew in.

Their overturned canoe was floating in the water off Mystery Island. A party of family members searched the lake and the surrounding area, but no trace of the twins or their dog was found.

Today's Highlights

President Roosevelt Welcomes Cary Grant to White House . . pg.2

Zoot Suits All the Rage pg.3

Movie Review: *Bambi* pg.5

Local Student Wins Award for Model of All 48 States pg.6

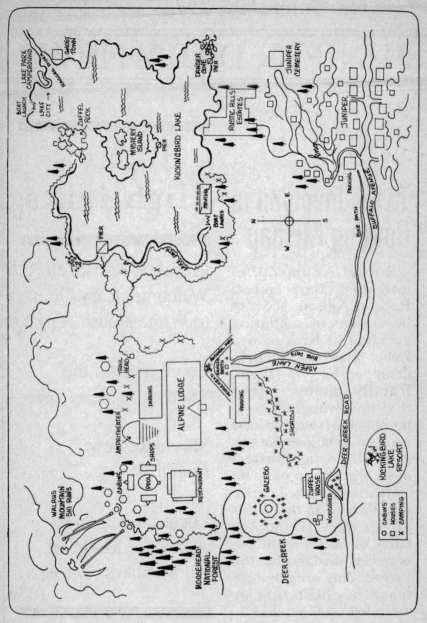

THE HAUNTED CAMPGROUND MYSTERY

1

Treasure Hunting

"**W**hat are you doing?" Robbie asked.

Beka glanced at her twin brother as she dashed about the attic, gathering her things. Being a ghost, she didn't have many "things" to gather.

The twin's growing pile of possessions happened to be items left behind at the Zuffel house by tourists who forgot to double-check closets and drawers before they departed.

With help from the ghost dog, Beka and Robbie would launch quick *treasure hunts* to claim all the "left behinds" before cleaning crews arrived and carted off their prizes.

To date, the twin's treasures included:

- pens, pencils, and notebooks (which Beka was gathering)
- a book about flowers (which Beka had practically memorized)
- sunglasses (three pairs; one broken)
- an address book (too bad for the owner)
- a pile of socks, mittens, sweaters, combs, and T-shirts (reminding Beka of the lost-and-found box at Hanover, their old elementary school)

Robbie was relaxing on his bunk with Thatch draped across his stomach. The *plink, plink, plink* of summer rain on the roof had lulled the ghost dog into an afternoon nap.

"I asked you a question," Robbie said, watching Beka with increasing curiosity. "What are you doing?"

Beka planted herself on the braided rug beside the bunk beds to check herself out in the mirror.

No reflection stared back.

Robbie laughed at her disappointed grimace.

She was wearing a sweater — one of their "finds."

Robbie sat up, making Thatch grumble-snore. "Why are you wearing a sweater in July?" he asked.

"It's chilly today because of the rain."

"Raz," he began, using their nickname formed from shared initials, "you're a *ghost*. You don't *get* chilly. Or hot, hungry, sleepy, wet, or *anything*."

Beka clutched a notebook in one arm, *pretending* she could see herself in the mirror. "I'm wearing a sweater because . . ." She paused, feeling embarrassed. "Well, because *they* are wearing sweaters."

"They?" Robbie repeated.

Beka jabbed a thumb toward the floor — their sign for downstairs.

"Oh, *them*. The giggling Mountain Adventure Club girls. Ho hum." Robbie faked a yawn. "You go join them. I'm staying right here, playing with Thatch, and reading the baseball book I *checked out* of the library."

His comment gave Beka mixed feelings. Normally she'd *want* Robbie to come along, yet she was *really* looking forward to being part of the girls' club, and . . . well . . . her brother *was* a boy.

"Gotta go," she chirped. "Our meeting's about to start. Ta-tah!"

"Our meeting?" Robbie echoed. "Ta-tah?"

Beka skipped across the attic and down the stairs.

With a reluctant "woof," Thatch roused himself

from his comfy spot, scrambled off the bunk, and trotted after Beka.

Sighing, Robbie plunked back down on his bunk.

Listening to the rain made him feel lonely — deserted by his dog and his sister. "A girls' club," he muttered. "Bah humbug. I think it's going to be a lo-o-o-ong weekend."

If only he knew how true his words would become.

2

Prissy, Cool, Funny, and Confused

Beka was first to arrive at the meeting —
scheduled for four o'clock on the sunporch.
The sunporch wasn't *really* a porch, but a room
added on to the back of the Zuffel house when the
twins were in kindergarten.

The walls were only waist-high, giving way to
windows that bordered three sides of the room.
The porch was the brightest, sunniest room in the
house — in summertime. In winter, it was the
coldest room because it wasn't heated.

Today, rain streaked the windowpanes, giving
a blurred appearance to everything in the backyard, and making the room gloomy and gray.

But Beka's mood was far from gloomy.

She knew what followed summer rainstorms:

bright sunshine warming the freshly washed hills and valleys of Kickingbird.

Eager for the meeting to start, Beka settled onto a sofa. Thatch sat at her feet, giving her a puzzled look that said, *"Why did I leave Robbie's cozy bunk to sit here in an empty room with you?"*

"Just wait," Beka said, patting his head. "They'll be here soon."

She opened the notebook, reminding herself to keep hold of it. If she let go, it would move into the "other world," and become visible to whoever might be looking — like one of the Mountain Adventure Club girls.

Beka had brought along the notebook to jot *impressions* of each girl — an idea borrowed from a book she'd stumbled across at the library in Juniper called *Writing Your Own Stories.*

At least *that's* what she planned to tell Robbie.

Her *real* reason for being here was because *she* was a "MAC girl," too. From the Raccoon Team. She'd even earned a whole bunch of Earth Pins.

She *belonged* in this room with the other MAC girls.

Only she didn't want Robbie to laugh at her.

Suddenly, the team leader bustled in, glanced at her watch, then shook her head, looking dismayed.

Beka waited for the leader to notice her and

exclaim, "Well, hello, young lady. Who are you?"

Beka *always* waited for people to do that, but of course, they never did.

While the woman peered at notes on a clipboard, Beka scribbled her impression:

Team Leader :

Dark ponytail with curly bangs.

Baggy denim pants (like people in the army wear).

Sweatshirt with the MAC girl logo on it.

A whistle on a chain around her neck.

~~Tall~~

Beka crossed out "Tall." She could do better than that. She tapped her pencil on the page, thinking, then wrote:

As tall as the backyard sunflowers in August.

7

Pleased, she read the sentence once more. Her third-grade teacher would have loved it, and given her a ★.

TWEEEET!

Beka jumped. She hadn't expected the lady to blow her whistle inside the house.

Thatch sprang to his feet.

Thunder shook the walls.

The dog pranced around the room, ready for action.

Then Beka realized it wasn't thunder. It was the sound of four MAC girls pounding down the stairs and racing to the sunporch.

They all burst in at once, jabbering so loudly Beka couldn't understand what anyone was saying.

Thatch acted as if he was ready to help — only he didn't know what all the commotion was about.

The leader waved her hand, threatening to blow the whistle again.

One by one, the girls noticed and stopped talking.

"Four o'clock means four o'clock," she told them.

"Sorry, Mrs. Galt," mumbled the girls.

"Sit," she ordered.

Thatch sat.

"Not you." Beka lunged to pull the ghost dog

out of the way before the girls sat on top of him.

The group formed a semicircle while the leader — Mrs. Galt — called roll, which Beka thought was dumb since there were only four girls.

"It helps me remember names," the lady told them.

While she welcomed everyone to the Kickingbird Lake Resort, Beka quickly jotted her impression of each girl:

1. Leah
Foofy blond hair. (How'd she get it to stick out like that?)
A Texas accent like Mr. Tavolott's. (Owner of the resort.)
White shorts and sweater. (Not a good color to wear if you want to go outside and have any fun at all.)

9

Beka recalled watching Leah wipe the floor clean with a hanky before she sat. Following advice from the writing book, she jotted a one-word impression of the girl: *Prissy*

2. *Rani*

Dark hair and skin. Pretty. (She reminded Beka of Thea Scranton, her best friend in second grade.)

Long T-shirt over leggings. Shirt says, "I'm the boss." Sweater tied around her waist.

One-word impression: Cool

Beka peeled off her own sweater and tied it around her waist, then continued:

3. *Amber*

Hair matches her name.

Dangly cat earrings and cat pin.

One-piece romper. (What they were called fifty years ago.)

One-word impression: Funny

4. *Paula*
   Everyone calls her "Crash". (Beka
   wasn't sure why.)

   *Short red hair — as tangled
   as the feathery fennel leaves
   growing by the back steps.*
   (Beka gave herself another ★.)

   *Braces
   Freckles — lots
   Wearing a MAC girl uniform.* (Niftier
   than the one Beka had worn.)

   One word-impression : Confused

Beka studied the girl's uniform: a striped tunic
in the MAC colors (walnut, berry, and pine) over
pine leggings, with the MAC logo decorating the
tunic.

Beka recalled *her* uniform: a walnut blouse and
shorts set, trimmed in berry, with *Mountain Adventure Club* on the pocket in fancy letters.

After roll call, Mrs. Galt hugged the clipboard

11

to her chest. "As you know, we are here for a special reason."

Beka stopped writing to listen.

"Each of you is a winner. Chosen to be here this weekend."

"We weren't *chosen*," Amber groaned. "It was a lottery. Fate. Chance. Bad luck."

The other girls snickered while Mrs. Galt acted appalled.

"Paula, your presence here is an honor."

"That's not Paula," Beka said. "It's Amber."

Amber didn't correct the leader's mistake.

Paula (Crash) looked wounded.

"Well, why couldn't our friends come?" Amber asked. "I mean . . ." She glanced at the others, but said no more.

"As members of the Coyote Team, you all know each other, don't you?"

The girls grumbled in agreement.

"It's *me* you don't know. I was chosen by lottery, too, out of all the MAC team leaders in the city. Does that make you feel better?"

Based on the girls' expressions, it didn't.

"Well, anyway," Mrs. Galt said, "I promise you a fun weekend."

"In the rain?" Rani complained.

The leader peered out the windows. "It's bound to stop sooner or later."

12

"Mah jacket isn't wahterproof," grumbled Leah.

Amber and Rani exchanged glances, trying not to laugh.

"Okay, okay." Mrs. Galt erased a few things on her clipboard, then filled in changes. "We might as well stay in the house tonight because of the rain. Besides, we've arrived too late to hike to Lake Park Campground before dark."

"Yea!" cheered the girls.

"Ta-tah!" threw in Leah.

Mrs. Galt waited for quiet to return. "In the morning, we'll get a fresh start. I'll bet Mr. Sun will be out by then."

"Mr. Sun?" echoed Beka.

"Mr. Sun?" mimicked Amber.

Mrs. Galt peered at the group over the top of her glasses while they giggled and nudged each other.

"Most importantly," she told them, "we're here to earn our Overnighter Earth Pins. Which ones have you chosen to work on?"

"The Camper Cooking Pin," Crash said.

Mrs. Galt motioned to the other girls.

"Ecology for me," Rani added.

"Snow Trekking," said Amber.

Everyone laughed.

"Wrong time of the year," Crash told her.

13

"No kidding." Amber made a goofy face. "I *meant* to say the Trail Blazer Pin."

"And Ah'm working on the Artistic Pin," Leah finished.

"Figures," Amber mumbled.

"Very good," Mrs. Galt exclaimed.

"Hey, what about me?" Beka jumped off the couch, riling up Thatch again. "I'll be working on a new pin, too," she told them. "It's called the Ghost Pin — and you guys all get to help . . . !"

3
Off-Limits

It didn't take Beka long to figure out why Paula was nicknamed *Crash*.

After Mrs. Galt ended the meeting, the group headed for the entry hall to claim their backpacks and sleeping bags.

Along the way, Crash:

1. Tripped on the edge of the hall carpet.
2. Jammed a finger while hoisting up her sleeping bag.
3. Stepped on the heel of Leah's white tennis shoes — which, according to Leah, ruined her "en-tar" weekend.

"Thatch," Beka whispered to the ghost dog. "Keep an eye on the redhead. I vote her the one who'll need the most rescuing."

Thatch padded ahead to sniff and nuzzle Crash, almost as if he knew what Beka was telling him.

Then Crash did something strange.

She flinched — just like she was reacting to the ghost dog!

"Whoa," Beka said. "Did you see that, puppy?"

Keeping Thatch away from people was impossible. But it wasn't a problem. Most people had no idea a ghost dog was tailing them, yet sometimes they reacted to a sudden burst of cold air, which the twins called *a ghost chill.*

While the girls pounded up the stairway, drowning out Mrs. Galt's orders and reminders, Crash stood frozen on the steps — shoulders tensed, eyes peeled.

"Paula, what's wrong?" asked Mrs. Galt.

"Um." Crash's face reddened. "Did you feel something just now?"

The leader yanked her glasses to the middle of her nose, peering over them as she studied the wide-eyed girl. "What exactly did you feel?"

Crash shrugged. "Probably nothing." Ducking her head, she followed the others to the second floor, Thatch and Beka on her heels.

16

"Dibs on this room!" hollered Rani.

"Hey, that's *my* room," Beka said. "My *old* room, I mean."

Rani and Amber plopped their packs onto the bed.

"You guys get the other room," Rani said, taking charge.

Crash and Leah found Robbie's old room.

In seconds, Leah was back, staring at Rani as though she'd told her to sleep outside in the rain. "Ya'll want me to sleep in a room with baseball posters on the wall?"

"What's wrong with baseball?" Amber asked.

Beka watched Leah's eyes take in her old room: frilly green and yellow curtains billowed at the windows. A matching comforter covered the bed. Old movie posters dotted the walls. A mini jukebox with a neon bubble tube sat on the desk next to Russian nesting dolls.

With a disgusted sigh, Leah returned to the "baseball room."

Beka settled into the rocker to watch Amber and Rani unpack.

"What's with all the noise?" came a voice from the doorway.

It was Robbie. "Sounds like the house is falling apart," he complained.

17

Thatch rushed to greet him. Robbie roughed up the dog's ears. "How long are these noisy MAC girls staying?"

"Just tonight," Beka answered. "Tomorrow we're going camping at Lake Park."

"We?"

"Yeah. You, me, Thatch, and the girls."

"Count me out," Robbie groaned. "What do *girls* know about camping?"

Beka scrambled across the room to slug him.

Only he was too quick.

Robbie was down the hall and halfway up the attic stairs before she and Thatch caught him.

"I was kidding," Robbie yelped. "Please don't tickle me."

"Tickling was *not* what I'd planned to do to you." Laughing, Beka curled her fingers into a fist. "How'd ya like a ghost punch?"

Thatch's bark echoed loudly in the narrow stairwell.

"Look what you've done." Robbie ran up the stairs to calm Thatch.

"Sorry, puppy." Beka wondered how the dog's hearty bark could sound so loud to them, yet not be heard by others in the house.

"He's confused," she added. "Whenever we chase each other, his loyalty is torn. He doesn't know which one of us to *save*."

Footsteps echoed below them on the steps. A light clicked on.

Rani peered up the stairway. "What's up here?"

"Nothing," Robbie snapped. "The attic is off-limits. Especially to MAC girls."

Even Beka agreed. Sharing her house with strangers had been hard at first, but as long as the attic remained theirs, she felt okay about sharing everything else.

Beka spread her feet apart, "blocking" the way as Amber and Rani took a few hesitant steps.

"Let's make Crash go up first," Rani whispered.

Amber looked eager to agree.

In seconds they were back, dragging a befuddled Crash to the stairwell.

"You can sleep in our room if you go to the third floor and tell us what's up there," Rani promised.

Crash's face lit up. "I can sleep in your room?"

"Sure," Amber agreed.

They shoved her up the stairs and closed the door.

"Hey!" Crash cried. "Leave it open!"

"Just run upstairs and see what's there," Rani ordered through the closed door.

Beka stood three steps above Crash. Robbie and Thatch were near the top.

A low growl rumbled in the ghost dog's throat.

19

"See?" Robbie said. "Even Thatch knows the attic belongs to us."

Crash took a few timid steps.

Beka wondered how "in tune" the girl was to ghosts. Some people could sense their presence, and some could not.

This one could.

"Go back, go back, go back," Beka chanted.

Crash's face, already pale in the dim light, drained of color altogether. Even her freckles paled.

Before Beka had time to say another word, Crash flew down the steps and out the door.

"Wow!" Beka glanced up the stairwell at her brother. "That was fast. Usually, it takes longer for me to *haunt* somebody. This girl's an easy mark."

"Ha," was all Robbie said.

"Hey," Beka added. "I've made up another Ghost Rule: *Some people can instantly sense our presence, but most cannot.*"

Pleased, Beka hurried down the stairs. Finding new Ghost Rules always made her happy.

The twins found Crash slumped over the hall banister, gasping for breath.

"Glory!" exclaimed Leah. "What happened?"

"I-I . . ." Crash sputtered, but couldn't get any words out.

20

"Oh, you're just teasing," Amber said. "You didn't see anything."

"Good show," Rani added. "You're quite an actress. As a matter of fact, you just gave me a great idea. After dinner, let's get ready for bed, then meet in our room, and tell ghost stories."

Crash sank to the floor as if she couldn't believe Rani's plan.

"Cool idea," Amber said.

"It's a silly idea," Leah snipped. "Grow up, ya'll, or Ah'm gonna tell Mrs. Galt."

"Mrs. G. won't care," Amber told her. "Sharing stories is one of the activities for earning the Storytelling Pin."

"Right," Rani agreed. "Just pretend you're working on a new Earth Pin in our room after dinner. Be there."

"*I'll* be there," Robbie answered. "I'll bet *we* know ghost stories you've never heard — since *we* are the ghosts in the stories!"

"Woof," agreed Thatch.

Beka gave her brother a sideways frown. "I thought you were spending the weekend in the attic because '*ho-hum MAC girls are boring.*'"

"Changed my mind," Robbie singsonged. "This

group is *far* from boring." Then he threw in his own *"Ta-tah!"*

"I told you so," Beka singsonged back to him.

She loved being right — almost as much as she loved making up new Ghost Rules.

4
A Spooky Story

After dinner, the group gathered upstairs in Beka's old bedroom.

Rani and Amber curled up on the bed.

Leah sat in the rocker, trying to rub the dirty mark off the back of her white tennis shoe with a soapy washcloth. Every few seconds, she glared at Crash.

Crash sat at the desk, looking stiff and uncomfortable.

The twins and Thatch sprawled on the carpet.

Mrs. Galt stayed downstairs in her own room — but not before issuing lots of orders about no loud talking and no staying up late.

"Are you really going to do it?" Crash asked in a tiny voice.

"Do what?" Amber yanked a pillow from under the comforter to lean against, punching it into place.

"Tell scary stories."

Rani *tsk*-sighed. "What's wrong with sharing spooky stories . . . in this strange house . . . all alone . . . with something evil lurking in the attic . . . and no one to protect us but — Mrs. G.!"

"*Stop*, ya'll!"

The twins howled. Amber was the only *live* one who shared their amusement.

"Let's talk about boys instead," Leah gushed.

The others groaned.

Beka straightened, suddenly interested. "Okay with me," she said.

Robbie joined the groaning.

"I'm serious, you guys," Crash cut in. "Ghost stories are too spooky when you, um, *believe* in them."

"You believe in ghosts?" Amber raised an eyebrow.

Crash shrugged. "Sometimes things happen . . ." Her voice trailed off. "I mean, some things are hard to explain."

"You *did* see something in the attic." Rani came to her knees. "What? Did you see a ghost?"

Everyone waited for Crash's answer.

She reached for a small vase of silk flowers on the desk and began to rearrange them. "I didn't *see* anything, but — don't you ever *feel* like something weird is going on?"

The girls shook their heads.

Rani knee-walked to the edge of the bed, closer to Crash. "Do you think this house is . . . haunted?"

"Eww-EEEEE-ewww," Amber moaned.

"Hey, that's *my* line," Robbie told her.

Crash returned the vase to its spot. "I'm saying I don't think it's a good idea to tell ghost stories in a house that has such a strange *feel* about it."

"Are you calling us strange?" Beka said. "I resent that."

"She must have ESP." Robbie nudged Thatch to his paws. "Let's test her." He made the ghost dog sit next to Crash's chair.

Instantly, the girl yanked her feet off the floor, tucking them beneath her legs.

"Mmm," Beka said, watching Crash peer around the room. Was she on guard for other *strange* things to happen?

"We can *always* talk about boys," Leah offered.

25

A look from the others silenced her.

Rani shivered as Robbie moved past her, returning to his place on the floor. "Close the window," she said. "It's getting cold in here."

Leah closed the window.

"Lock it," Crash ordered.

Leah locked it.

"Now." Rani resumed a comfortable position, sprawled across the bed. "Who wants to tell the first story?"

"You do." Amber kicked her with a stockinged foot. "This was your idea; you go first."

"Okay," Rani chirped, then grinned wickedly. "I have *lots* of stories. My grandfather teaches folklore at a university in Calcutta. He's always sending me books on myths and legends from India."

"So tell us," Amber urged.

Rani rolled onto her back a moment to think. "Okay, here's a good one." Sitting up, she began. "One night, a young rajah was — "

"What's a rajah?" Amber interrupted.

"An Indian prince," Rani explained. "The rajah had gone hunting, and stayed too long in the forest. On his way home, the sky grew dark, and the young man grew tired."

Beka leaned forward, listening. She'd read just

about every ghost story on the shelves of the Sugarberry Library in Juniper. Maybe this was one she already knew.

"He came upon a palace, so he stopped to spend the night. But no one seemed to live there. He wondered why such a beautiful palace would be standing empty."

Leah stopped fussing with her tennis shoe to listen.

"How'd he get in?" Amber asked in a hushed voice.

"The drawbridge was down, so he rode his horse right into the center of the courtyard. Then . . ."

Rani stopped until they all asked, "Then *what*?"

"Then the drawbridge began to close by itself. *Cre-e-e-a-a-ak!*"

Thatch scrambled to his feet, lifting one ear to Rani's creaking.

"He got off his horse and went up the palace steps. The door began to open by itself. *Cre-e-e-a-a-ak!*"

"Woof!"

Robbie chuckled. "I think they need to oil the hinges at this palace."

Crash hopped from the chair to sit on top of the desk.

Further away from Thatch? Beka wondered.

Robbie moved to the door.

"You can't leave now," Beka said. "Rani's just getting to the good part."

"I'm not leaving." Robbie stopped by the door and rested his hand on the light switch.

All he had to do was concentrate on the switch until he could move it. Then he'd be able to turn off the light.

"Clever," Beka told him.

"The rajah walked into a great hall. A feast had been laid out on a long table. There was only one chair. Sitting down, he ate his fill."

Leah gave a little gasp. "And nobody was *ther-rah?*"

"Nobody was *ther-rah,*" Rani answered, imitating Leah's accent.

Amber slid under the bed covers. "Go on," she urged.

"All of a sudden, as the rajah was finishing his dinner, a voice — "

CLICK!

Darkness claimed the room.

Screams rattled the windows, but nobody ran.

Thatch's howls competed with the screams.

"Good show, Raz," Beka hollered over the barking and screaming.

Moments later, the light clicked on.

Mrs. Galt appeared. She'd removed the band from her ponytail. Her hair curled around the shoulders of a pink nightgown. She gaped at the wide-eyed MAC girls, all huddled on top of the bed. "What's going on?"

"Nothing." Leah's voice was trembly, giving away her fear.

"It's lights-out time," the leader told them.

"No kidding." Amber's joke received a few weak laughs.

Quickly, Leah explained what had happened.

"Well, this is an old house," Mrs. G. said. "Maybe the wiring is faulty in places. The downstairs lights seem fine."

"Whew," sighed Amber, relieved to hear a logical explanation.

"I'll report it to Mr. Tavolott, just to be safe. Meanwhile," she added, "let's settle down and get some sleep. Big day tomorrow."

After Mrs. Galt left, the girls stared at each other's scared faces.

"Um," Crash began. "Rani? Remember when you told me I could sleep in your room if I went up the attic stairs?"

"Yes."

"Well, I did it, so I can sleep here, right?"

"You didn't go all the way to the top," Rani argued.

Amber nudged her. "It's okay. Maybe we should all stay in the same room. It seems safer. Except *you* guys have to sleep on the floor."

"The *floor-ah*?!" Leah acted shocked. "Ah can't sleep on the *floor-ah*."

"Fine," Rani told her. "Crash can move in with us, and you can stay in the baseball-poster room all by yourself."

That worked.

Five minutes later, two sleeping bags were rolled out on the floor, and everyone was in bed.

Thatch stretched out next to Crash, who completely disappeared inside her bag, head and all.

Amber clicked off the light. After a few moments of darkness, she whispered, "Hey, Rani. Finish the rajah's story."

"Noooooo!" wailed the others.

Rani laughed. "I'll finish it. But not tonight. I'll wait until tomorrow when we're all alone in the deep dark forest."

Someone groaned. "At least we'll be away from this house — just in case it *is* haunted."

"It is," Robbie announced. "But I have bad news for you. So is the deep dark forest."

5
Ferry to the Far Side

In the morning, Mrs. Galt locked the front door of the Zuffel house and hurried down the veranda steps to survey the Coyote Team.

The girls stood at attention for inspection. All wore backpacks with sleeping bags strapped to the bottoms. Cooking items and food had been evenly distributed.

Rani was wearing the niftiest sunglasses Beka had ever seen. The frames were engraved with tiny rainbows, which sparkled in the sun.

"Maybe Rani will leave them behind so I can have them," Beka whispered to herself — then felt guilty for having such a greedy thought.

Amber wore a cat T-shirt and a cat charm bracelet.

Leah was dressed head to toe in white, because, as she'd pointed out, *"White sets off mah hair."*

Crash wore jeans instead of shorts like the others, plus a long-sleeved shirt and a baseball cap.

Beka wondered if Crash was fighting the sun to keep from getting more freckles. If so, the score was: Freckles — nine zillion; Crash — 0.

Robbie was playing chase with Thatch across the front lawn.

Beka started to join them, but joined the inspection line instead, wishing *she* had a backpack. Plus, hiking shorts and kneesocks and boots. *And* rainbow sunglasses.

"At ease," Mrs. Galt told them, but they'd already begun to wander around the front drive, talking and giggling over . . . what? Beka had missed their private joke. She moved closer so she wouldn't miss anything else.

Mrs. Galt unfolded a map, mumbling about starting off in the right direction. She squinted at the sun, which was trying to break through the remains of yesterday's rain clouds.

"East!" she exclaimed, pointing toward Juniper.

"Right," Beka agreed. "Why don't you let *me* lead you to Lake City? I know the quickest route."

Mrs. Galt, wearing sensible shoes with her baggy army pants, headed down the drive to Deer Creek Road, then turned east.

The girls followed.

Rani and Amber walked together. Then came Leah. Crash trailed behind.

"Hey!" Beka waved at Robbie and Thatch. "Are you two coming?"

Robbie raced to catch up. "I wouldn't miss this for anything — not even a hot patty melt at Blaze's Burgers. These girls are fun to haunt."

"We're going along to *help* them, not *haunt* them," Beka said, imitating Mrs. Galt's tone of voice.

"What's wrong with a little of both?"

Robbie's comment filled Beka's mind with lots of possibilities. Yet, she didn't want to *haunt* the MAC girls; she wanted to *be* a MAC girl.

"Why are you bringing your notebook?" Robbie asked, looking puzzled.

Beka had brought it along in case she wanted to jot more notes about the girls for her future stories. "Um, just because," she said, not giving him a reason to tease her.

Thatch raced ahead to "help" Mrs. Galt.

At the fork in the road, the leader paused, fumbling with the map.

"Turn left, turn left, turn left," Beka chanted.

"I guess we keep heading straight," she said.

"Noooo." Beka tried to tap Mrs. G. on the shoulder, but her hand went *through* the leader.

Thatch barked. Even *he* knew the right direction.

"I think we go left here," Crash offered.

"Thank you," said Beka.

"How do you know?" Mrs. Galt asked.

Crash tripped over a rock on the side of the road. "Um, I just have a feeling."

"Ha," Amber said. "You mean, you saw the sign."

"What sign?"

Half hidden by bushes was a marker, pointing left. It read: *To Kickingbird Lake and Moosehead National Park.*

"Oh," said Crash and Mrs. Galt.

The group's fearless leader put away her map and followed signs all the way to the entry arch into Moosehead.

The ghost twins led the way to Kickingbird Lake. Today, the water looked gray, reflecting clouds floating above.

"Make a choice, girls," chirped Mrs. Galt. "Do we hike around the lake to the campground? Or take a ferry boat?"

"Ferry boat!" chimed four voices.

Beka grimaced. She avoided going out on the

lake whenever possible. It all had to do with another cloudy summer afternoon fifty-some years ago.

Since she couldn't voice her opinion, Beka boarded the ferry with the others. She climbed to the top deck as the boat skimmed the surface of the water on its way to the far side of the lake.

Halfway across, the ferry passed Mystery Island. Suddenly the sun burst through the clouds, changing gray water into brilliant blue.

The sight lifted Beka's mood immensely.

Soon the ferry slowed, chugging into the cove where Ragged River emptied into Kickingbird.

The twins weren't as familiar with this side of the lake, since it was such a long hike from their house.

As the ferry approached the pier, Beka was surprised to see a bustling main street in what used to be the tiny town of Lake City.

Sitting on the north side of the river was a much larger town than she remembered. Shops and cafes lined the shore. Last time Beka was here, there wasn't even a dock.

"Nifty," Robbie said, joining her at the railing. "There's lots to do here." His gaze scanned the shore. "Oh, look," he added. "There's another MAC girl."

Robbie pointed up the street. At the corner was a post office. A girl wearing a Mountain Adventure Club uniform stood out front, watching the ferry dock.

Beka shielded her eyes to get a better look. "That's weird," she mumbled.

"What?"

"The girl's uniform. It's so old-fashioned. That's what MAC girls wore years ago." Even the girl's long braids seemed out-of-date.

A whistle blared, announcing the arrival of the Kickingbird Ferry to Lake City. Passengers lined up at the stairs to disembark.

Robbie grabbed Thatch's collar to steer him safely *through* the crowd.

"Coming, Bek?" he called.

"In a second," she told him. Something about the lone MAC girl standing there watching the ferry dock struck Beka as odd.

Especially since she felt as though the girl was looking directly at *her*.

6

Lake City

"**C**an we look in some of the shops, Mrs. Galt?" Rani asked as the girls gathered on the dock. "Yes!" chimed the others.

"We're not here to shop," their leader reminded them. "You can shop at home."

"But I promised my little sister I'd bring her a souvenir," Amber argued.

"And Ah'm dying for a lemonade," Leah added.

The twins laughed at the weary expression on Mrs. Galt's face.

"She looks real sorry she was chosen to escort *this* group," Robbie muttered.

Beka agreed, grasping Thatch's collar to keep him from dashing off. He seemed eager to head in the direction of the mysterious MAC girl.

Beka turned again to look for the girl. There she was, peeking around the wall of the post office. Didn't she want to be seen? Where was the rest of her group?

"We have a long hike ahead of us," Mrs. Galt began in a firm tone. "And it will take a while to set up camp. After that, we'll pick our projects for this afternoon. Next, we'll fix lunch, and *all* have a lemonade." She winked at Leah.

"Tomorrow, on our return trip," she continued, "we can shop for souvenirs."

The girls reluctantly agreed.

"You'll all earn your Overnighter Pin this weekend, in addition to others you're working on," Mrs. Galt told them. "Isn't that exciting?"

"Yes!" exclaimed Crash.

Beka noticed that the others couldn't hide their excitement as they quickly pulled on their backpacks and got ready to hike into the hills.

Earning pins *was* exciting. Beka remembered all the ones she'd clipped onto her uniform. There'd been at least fifteen.

"Here's the plan." Mrs. Galt spread a map onto the railing of the pier. "Trails to the campgrounds start behind the post office, which is . . ." Pausing, she peered down the street.

"You're looking the wrong way," Beka told her.

The girls helped, scouting the area.

"There it is!" Rani hollered.

"Oh." Mrs. Galt frowned at the map, then at the post office. "Why of course. It's thataway." She tried to fold the map, but gave up, stuffing it inside her jacket. "Let's go."

The group meandered down Lake Street, stopping to gaze into shop windows, while Mrs. Galt tried to hurry them along.

Behind the post office lay a town park, bordering a small cemetery.

In the center of the park was a marble monument honoring the pioneers who'd first settled the Kickingbird hills. A garden maze with square-trimmed bushes zigzagged around the statue.

A ranger Beka had never seen before was stationed at an information booth. He handed out brochures and chatted with Mrs. Galt, who asked him to draw arrows and circles on her map so she'd know where to go.

Beka wandered around the park, searching for the strange MAC girl.

She was nowhere in sight.

"Where'd she go?" Robbie asked, catching up with her. "I figured the park would be overflowing with MAC girls, but she seems to be by herself."

Thatch was busy covering every inch of the

park, nose down, tail *not* wagging, which is what his tail did whenever he was concerned about something. *Not* a good sign.

"Time to move out," called Mrs. Galt.

Leah was taking pictures of the pioneer statue. Amber and Rani were dashing through the garden maze, trying to find the exit, and Crash was wandering among the grave markers in the cemetery.

At Mrs. Galt's command, they all gathered on a bridge that curved across a trickling stream. The bridge marked the start of a path leading to Lake Park Campground in the hills above town.

As they hiked, the twins listened to the girls jabbering and teasing. Thatch chased the summer insects dive-bombing the group.

No one paid any attention to the bugs — except Leah, who'd pulled her white sweater over her head for protection.

"Isn't this fun?" Beka nudged her brother. "You love hiking and camping."

"Okay, okay." Robbie shoved her hand away. "You were right, and I was wrong. I'm having a fun weekend — in spite of the MAC girls."

Beka gave him a smug grin.

A few minutes later, Robbie stopped. "Hey, what happened to Thatch?"

Beka remembered seeing the ghost dog stop his bug chasing, and charge past them down the path.

She twirled to look behind, but trees and rocks blocked her view of the winding trail.

"I thought he was right behind us."

"Thatch!" Robbie shouted. "Here, boy!"

The twins waited, but the dog did not appear.

Hopping onto a jagged rock, Beka climbed as high as she could to peer over the treetops.

The sight on the path below made her heart skitter. "Yikes," she whispered.

"What is it?" Robbie hollered. "Is Thatch all right?"

"He's fine," Beka called back. "But he isn't alone."

Trudging up the hill behind the ghost dog came the elusive MAC girl.

7

Now You See Her;
Now You Don't

"Let's go check her out," Robbie said, sounding determined.

Beka hopped off the rock. "But we'll lose track of the other girls."

Robbie had already broken into a run. He hollered back over his shoulder. "The ranger said this path leads to the campsites. The only way we can lose the girls is if they stray from the path."

"Ha," Beka scoffed. "Remember who their leader is. Mrs. Galt doesn't know north from south, or up from down."

Robbie was already out of earshot.

Beka hurried after him.

A minute later, Thatch flew around a bend, galloping toward them.

The twins put on the brakes.

Thatch looked at them as if he wanted to say *"Guess what? I found a new friend."*

As they waited for the girl to appear, Beka's stomach coiled into a knot. "She's bound to walk right through us, and keep on going. We won't know any more about her than we do already."

Robbie's answer was a shrug. "So, maybe we can follow her."

"How can we follow *her* when she's following *us?*"

"Following the MAC girls, you mean."

Another minute passed. The girl never came around the bend.

Thatch lifted one ear and gazed at the trail, as if he, too, was wondering what happened to her.

"I don't get it." Robbie started downhill. "Let's look for her."

"It's no use," Beka muttered, balking at a further search. "We should have run into her by now; she was right behind Thatch."

Robbie snatched at a butterfly, but it fluttered through his hand. "How could she disappear so fast? And why?"

"Maybe she *knows* about us," Beka offered.

"How could she know?"

"*Crash* knows."

"Well, sort of." Robbie shot her a look of disbelief. "Crash had a hunch something strange was happening at the Zuffel house, but she doesn't know about *us*."

"Here, Thatch." Beka knelt, patting his scruffy head. "Find . . . the . . . girl." She spoke slowly, wondering if the ghost dog understood.

Thatch stayed frozen, ears raised, nose lifted — almost as if someone *else* was telling him to stay put.

"Aw, forget it," Robbie said. "She's probably a tourist, and she's gone back to Lake City to find her family."

His reasoning sounded logical.

"Come on, Bek. If we hurry, we can catch the others in no time."

Beka followed, but couldn't resist stopping every few minutes to glance behind at the winding trail.

Meeting up with the Coyote Team was easy, thanks to the steep climb. Steep climbs made people go slower, but didn't bother ghosts at all.

Mrs. Galt was still in the lead. Followed by Crash.

Rani and Amber trailed behind, trading jokes. Like:

What do you get if you cross a mouse
with an elephant?
(Cats who are very, very worried.)

And:

Why did the bunny go to the hospital?
(To have a hoperation.)

Leah brought up the rear, practically tiptoeing,
trying to keep her white shoes clean. But it was
a losing battle. After yesterday's rain, mud had
claimed the path. Now it was mush.

Finally they reached the top. The muddy path
became a paved trail, winding in and out of
postcard-perfect campsites — all empty.

"Whoa, nobody else is here." Beka had expected
the hilltop to be crowded with campers.

"The ranger said this campground was reserved
for youth groups," Robbie told her. "Everyone
else camps along Ragged River."

The twins and Thatch inspected the area — the
twins, by foot; Thatch, by nose.

"If no other campers show up," Beka said,
thinking out loud, "the girls will be out here in
the boondocks all by themselves."

45

"So what?" Robbie wiggled his eyebrows menacingly. "They'll be easier to scare."

Beka read the directions on the freshwater pump, thinking how good a cup of icy mountain water would taste right now.

Robbie pretended to pump the well.

Beka knew he could really do it if he concentrated hard enough. Maybe he was saving his performance for later — after dark.

"How's this?" Mrs. Galt called from one end of the camping area.

"Too *fahr* from the bathrooms," Leah hollered.

Mrs. Galt moved closer to the rest-room hut.

"How's this?"

"Better," Leah said, "but now it's a hike to the *wahter* pump."

Mrs. Galt took off her pack, letting it *flump* to the ground. "*This* is where we'll stay." Her voice didn't invite more arguments.

Beka stopped at a fat log. Sitting down, she watched the sudden flurry of activity around the campsite. A hollowed-out spot underneath the log made a perfect hiding place for her notebook. Now she wouldn't have to hold on to it all night.

The girls rolled out mats for sleeping bags, then organized their belongings.

Mrs. Galt was the only one with a tent. Crash helped set it up.

Amber covered a picnic table with a plastic cloth, placing rocks on each corner so the breeze wouldn't whip it away.

Rani set out bread and sandwich meats and spreads. Leah poured a cup of lemonade for everyone.

"Before we eat," Mrs. Galt said, "let's form a Sister Circle."

As if on cue the girls gathered around the rock fireplace, grasping hands.

"Ohhh," Beka whined in a tiny voice. "Wait for me." She sidestepped around the circle, trying to get in.

"Woof!" Thatch barked, sensing her dismay.

"Raz, you can't join in, so don't even try."

Robbie copped Beka's seat on the log, grabbing Thatch to keep him away from the lunch meat lying unguarded on the picnic table — too tempting for a ghost dog to resist.

"Darn," Beka whimpered. She hated being left out. Giving her best pout, she stationed herself behind Rani, and *pretended* to be part of the circle.

"Paula, will you lead us in the Sister Code?" Mrs. Galt asked.

Crash looked pleased.

The girls raised their clasped hands to the sun. (What there was of it.)

Beka raised her hands, too.

"We will honor our families," Crash began, while the girls (and ghost) joined in. "We will serve our country, gain knowledge, and respect nature. This is the MAC Sister Code."

The girls cheered and hugged each other.

"They changed the code," Beka blurted. "It was different when I was a MAC girl."

"A *lot* of things have changed since then," Robbie reminded her.

The girls stayed in the circle to talk about their weekend projects. Leah found a towel to sit on so she wouldn't dirty her white shorts.

Beka drifted away from the group. She sat on the log beside Robbie, who tried to cheer her up by listing all the things that had changed between "then" and "now."

Suddenly, the words, "What's the matter?" caught the twin's attention.

The question was directed at Crash from Amber.

Crash had jumped to her feet, and was scrutinizing the campsite.

"Do you think she's sensing our presence again?" Beka asked.

"No." Robbie's voice sounded funny. "I think she's sensing *her* presence."

The shock on Robbie's face made Beka afraid

to turn her head and see what was causing such a strange reaction.

She forced herself to look.

Striding across the campground, glaring at them with an angry scowl, came the mysterious MAC girl.

8

The Mystery Girl

The girl strode past the Coyote Team's Sister Circle, straight toward the log on which Robbie and Beka were sitting.

She planted herself in front of them, hands firmly on her hips. "Who are you?" she demanded. "And what are you doing here?"

Beka was so shocked, she couldn't move. She stared at the girl's walnut-colored jeans and pine T-shirt, with berry "twig" letters: MAC. The uniform was different from the one Beka had worn, and *way* different from those of today.

"Are you talking to *us?*" Robbie asked.

Beka thought it a dumb thing to say, but since no one *ever* talked to them, his question was better than anything she could come up with.

All Beka's mind could register was the fact that the other girls weren't even *aware* of the person who'd just invaded their campsite.

Well, Crash had reacted, but even she'd sat down and resumed chatting with Leah.

Hearing a distant *yip*, Beka turned to see Thatch zooming back from his latest adventure to sniff and nuzzle the intruder.

The mystery girl petted the ghost dog, cooing to him in a soft tone. Beka realized the two had met before — on the path.

She finally got her mouth to work. "Are you a . . . a ghost?" she stammered.

Robbie *tsked* at her question as if it was rude.

In answer, the girl whipped around and marched toward the fire circle.

The Coyote Team was still discussing their Earth Pins and how they planned to earn them.

The girl walked *through* Amber and stood in the middle of the circle. "Hello," she said to them. "My name is Callie Lopez, from the Moose Team."

The other girls kept talking, ignoring the girl who the twins could see as clearly as everyone else — and who could see *them* in return.

"Crimeny!" Robbie jumped to his feet, acting as though he didn't know whether to shake the girl's hand or run away from her.

Giving the twins a smug grin, Callie walked

back through Amber to the log. "Does that answer your question?" she asked, yanking on one of her braids.

Beka forced her legs to stand. Nothing had shocked her *this* much since . . . well, since she'd discovered that *she* was a ghost.

"How did you know about us?" Robbie asked.

"I've been watching you. Ever since you sailed into Lake City."

Beka recalled spotting Callie from the ferry, and how she'd felt as if the girl was looking directly at her. Obviously, she *had* been.

The MAC girl petted Thatch again. "I've been watching you *and* your dog."

Her voice sounded wistful. Did the girl wish *she* had a ghost dog, too?

"This is my, um, territory," Callie said. "You shouldn't be here; you'll mess up everything if I have to . . ." She stopped, obviously not wanting to tell them too much.

"Your *territory*?" Robbie repeated. "You mean, ghosts have territories assigned to them to haunt?"

"I don't believe that," Beka scoffed, unsure whether or not to trust the girl.

"No. I didn't mean it like that." Callie paused to watch the other girls. They'd disbanded their

Sister Circle, and were gathering around the picnic table for lunch.

"I guess I'll have to tell you my story," she continued. "But first, *you* tell *me* why you're here and when you became ghosts."

The twins quickly filled her in on that long-ago summer afternoon, the canoe trip from Mystery Island, the stormy weather, and their "mishap," as people later called it.

They told her about returning to their home three years later, finding it deserted, moving in, and . . . well, that was just about the whole story.

"Your turn," Beka urged, eager to hear how another girl her age woke up one morning as a ghost.

Callie sat beside them on the log. "Are you two here all the time?" she asked.

"We *three* are," Robbie said, including Thatch, who'd stationed himself by the picnic table, waiting for someone to drop a scrap of food.

"Well, I'm not," Callie said. "I only come back when I'm needed."

"When you're needed?" Beka didn't understand.

"This is where my, um, *mishap* occurred," she said, borrowing their word. "And I find myself here only when other MAC girls need help — one way or another. It's only happened about three times in the past . . ." She squinted at the sky, thinking. "In the past thirty years."

"Wow," Beka said, glad they were "around" all the time instead of popping in and out of "this world."

"Last time," Callie continued, "I saved a third-grader who'd gotten stung by a swarm of bees while on a picnic with her team."

Beka was afraid to ask the next question, but curiosity made her. "So what happened to *you?* I mean, how did you become a ghost?"

Callie stood, flipping her braids behind her shoulders. "Come with me," she told them. "And I'll *show* you what happened."

Beka glanced at her brother. *This is creepy!* she whispered in her mind.

Robbie nodded, as if he'd received her silent message.

Without another word, the twins followed their fellow ghost away from the circle of empty campsites, off into the shadowy forest.

9

Not a Bad Job for a Ghost

Beka gave a quick glance over one shoulder as she followed Callie.

The MAC girls — well-guarded by the ghost dog — were still eating lunch. Of course, Thatch was there for doggie reasons.

Callie led them up and down a few hills, then around a wooded rise. Weaving through trees, she finally stopped at a low cement wall, banked against the base of a cliff.

"See this?" She touched the wall, then pointed to a pile of tumbled down bricks and another wall a couple of dozen yards away.

"This used to be a huge cabin," she told them. "Part of Lake Park Campground. MAC girls from all over the country came here to stay.

"I came for a weekend retreat during the summer I was ten." She gave them an embarrassed look. "Well, I guess I still *am* ten."

Beka could relate to her words. *She* would always be eleven.

Callie circled the cabin's foundation. "My best friend Debby Ward and I won the trip to Lake Park because we earned more Earth Pins that year than anyone else in the Moose team."

"So, what happened to the cabin?" Robbie blurted, acting impatient.

Beka jabbed him in the ribs. He could never stand still for long explanations.

Robbie returned her frown with an innocent shrug.

"The cabin burned down," Callie told them, "in the middle of the night. I never knew if it'd been struck by lightning, or if lightning sparked a fire in the surrounding trees."

She gestured toward overhanging branches shading the foundation. There was no evidence the trees had ever been on fire — but, of course, they'd had many summers to grow back.

"All I remember," Callie told them, "is a terrible thunderstorm. The lights blinked off and the phones went dead. Next, there was a horrible crash of thunder, and fireworks seemed to burst inside the cabin.

"Debby and I were in an upstairs bedroom. Everyone was shouting at us to run outside. Debby wanted to find her necklace first, because she'd just gotten it for her birthday.

"I-I didn't wait. I got out of there. Then I couldn't find Debby. It scared me. I thought she was still searching for her necklace, so I ran back inside to help her."

Beka had more or less figured out the rest of the story. Running back into a burning house was *never* a good idea.

"Debby had panicked, and couldn't find her way out, so I took her the way I'd gone — down the stairs and out an open window."

Callie paused to heave a sigh. "Debby dropped her necklace when she climbed out the window. She started crying, so I went in after it, and . . ."

Sighing, Callie somberly studied the area, as if picturing what it looked like on that terrible night.

"I knew it was silly to go back for the necklace. Debby begged me not to, but it was so *close*. Grabbing it and climbing outside should have been easy, but my timing was off. The roof collapsed, and I was trapped."

Quiet filled the summer afternoon.

"I'm sorry," Beka finally said.

"Oh, well, you get over it." Callie gave Beka a playful shove. "Right?"

Beka nodded, amazed that Callie's hand didn't go through her arm, but made solid contact.

Callie climbed four cement steps, leading to a porch that was no longer there. She made a goofy face to show them she was fine. "Looking out for others isn't a bad job for a ghost."

The twins laughed.

Now Beka felt at ease with Callie, and knew she could trust the "fifth MAC girl."

"So, now," Callie continued, "all I have to do is figure out why I came back this time. I suspect it's because one of the girls in the Coyote Team is going to do something risky — or dumb — and may need a little ghost help."

"My money's on Crash," Robbie offered.

"Crash?" Callie repeated.

"The redhead," Beka explained. "She seems to be the most accident-prone."

Callie hopped off the steps. "Maybe we should get back to camp. Someone might be needing me right now."

Without a backward glance, Callie headed into the trees. "I'm sorry I was nasty to you guys at first," she said. "I've never run into other ghosts before, and I thought you two were trying to take over my job."

"Maybe four MAC girls and their leader are more than *one* ghost can handle," Beka told her.

Callie agreed. "Could be an interesting night."

Back at camp, the girls were packing away food, piling up paper plates for tonight's fire, and cleaning the table.

"Here are more scraps for the birds and squirrels," Mrs. Galt said.

Amber placed the leftovers on a paper towel and hurried to the base of a sycamore tree to deposit the food. "Hey!" she called. "The stuff I left here three seconds ago is already gone."

"Wow," said Rani. "Those were some hungry squirrels."

"Thatch!" Robbie hollered.

The ghost dog peeked around the sycamore, licking his snout.

"You're stealing food from the animals." Robbie shook a finger at his dog. "Get over here."

Thatch was torn, but finally obeyed.

"Ready?" Mrs. Galt asked when the campsite was clean.

The girls assembled around their leader for directions. "Let me hear where you're off to so I can keep track of everyone." She attached a piece of paper to her clipboard. "Leah?"

"Ah'll be looking for the perfect nature scene to sketch in charcoal." Leah held up her drawing pad. "It's one of mah activities for the Artistic Pin."

Mrs. Galt jotted a note to herself. "Rani?"

"I'll be mapping out an ecosystem to study for the Ecology Pin. It has to be sixteen paces by sixteen paces. I think I'll head . . ." Pausing, she scanned the area. "That way."

"North," Mrs. Galt said, making a note.

"No, ma'am, I think it's south."

Mrs. Galt acted flustered as she erased her mistake. "Very good, Rani. Next, please. Amber?"

"I'll be blazing a new trail from here to the banks of Ragged River. It's about two miles."

"Terrific," Mrs. Galt said. "Paula?"

"I'm staying here," Crash answered. "First, I'll build a fire. That's one of the activities for the Camper Cooking Pin. Then, I'll fix dinner for everyone."

The girls cheered.

Their reaction made Crash's face turn pink, but Beka thought she looked pleased.

"Off to work," ordered their leader. "And please be careful."

The girls scattered.

"So, how do we know which one to follow?" Robbie asked.

"I'm not sure." Callie frowned after each girl, as if trying to guess which one needed protecting.

"Maybe we should split up," Beka suggested. "I'll follow Rani. Rob, you go with Leah."

"Gee, thanks." He made a face.

Beka ignored him. "And Callie, you trail Amber."

"Great idea," Callie said. "But what about Crash? I thought you said she was accident-prone."

"She's staying here at camp. With Mrs. Galt. I don't think we need to worry about her."

"Good point," Robbie muttered, heading after Leah. "One last question," he called. "Who gets Thatch?"

Thatch was beside himself, scurrying after one girl, dashing back to camp, then sniffing out the direction of another.

With a confused whine, he finally gave up trying to keep track of them all. Scampering toward the fire circle where Crash was arranging tinder, the ghost dog plopped down and closed his eyes.

"When in doubt, take a nap," Beka laughed. "I guess Crash gets her own personal guard after all."

With that, the three ghosts hurried in opposite directions to watch over their "assigned" MAC girl.

10
A Somber Warning

Beka picked her way through uneven terrain, sprinkled with unexpected rocks, and covered with patches of buffalo grass and prickly mountain cactuses.

Rani was avoiding the numerous trails, zigzagging here and there, as she searched for the perfect place to map out her ecosystem.

Beka wondered what an ecosystem was.

The heavy scent of sage filled the air. Bees hummed in rhythm, popping in and out of pink flowers dotting the bushes.

As many times as she'd read the flower book — one of the treasures left behind at the Zuffel house — Beka didn't know what kind of bushes they were — although she should have known.

Rani finally stopped in a cozy meadow, bordered on three sides by trees and on the fourth by a narrow stream.

Beka was glad she stopped. Wandering too far off the marked trails wasn't a good idea, even for a MAC girl.

Dumping her notebook onto a flat rock, Rani yanked a baseball cap from her back pocket and pulled it on. Then she started off, taking long strides. "One, two, three, four, five, six, seven, eight."

Stopping, she pulled a flagged stake from her pocket and shoved it into the ground.

Making a ninety-degree turn to the left, Rani counted sixteen paces, and planted another stake. Left turn, sixteen paces. And again. One more turn, and eight paces brought her back to her notebook.

Next, Rani sketched a map of her ecosystem, then wandered inside the area, making notes about the flowers, plants, insects, and any small animals darting across her path. (Beka peeked over her shoulder to read the notes.)

After a while, Beka grew tired of watching. She found a shady spot to rest — smack in the middle of Rani's ecosystem.

Lying on her back, Beka gazed at the clouds dotting the blue sky, watching them form into familiar shapes, one after the other.

Beka sat up. How long had she been napping? Or rather, *floating*, as ghosts did instead of sleeping.

Rani was gone. So were the red-flagged stakes.

The sun was deep in the western sky.

Beka jumped to her feet. "Rats." Had the girl gone back to camp? Or further into the forest. "I'm not a very good ghost guard," she mumbled.

After a quick stretch, Beka hurried back to camp, hoping she'd find Rani there. Along the way, she made up excuses for losing track of "her girl" — just in case Robbie and Callie gave her a hard time.

Yes, Rani was at camp. Beka felt relieved, yet flustered at having lost track of the one she was supposed to be protecting.

Mrs. Galt and the others sat in the shade of the sycamore, comparing notes on their experiences. Thatch lay sprawled in the middle of the group. He was snoring so loudly, Beka was surprised no one could hear him.

Crash was at the fire circle, still trying to build a roaring fire. Had she been at it this long?

Robbie and Callie sat at the picnic table. Leah's charcoal sketch lay on display between them. It was a birds-eye view of Lake City from the campground.

Beka thought it was pretty good, although she didn't think Kickingbird Lake's shoreline was as squiggly as Leah had sketched it. (She probably drew the picture standing up to keep her white jeans from getting dirty. . . .)

"So glad you could join us," Robbie called when he saw her.

"We were just wondering if *you* were the one who needed saving," Callie teased.

Beka tried to cover her embarrassment with a pouty look. "Weren't you the least bit worried about me?"

"You're a ghost," Robbie chuckled. "Why should I worry?"

She gave him a *look*, while Callie laughed.

"When's dinner?" Amber called. "I'm starving."

Crash fanned the puny flames. "Soon," she called back.

Beka was beginning to feel sorry for the red-head. "Did anything, um, *unusual* happen while I was gone?" Secretly, she hoped whatever "needed to be done" had been done, so she could relax and enjoy the rest of the weekend.

"Not yet," Callie said, dodging a sparrow who flew straight at her face.

"We don't *want* anything unusual to happen," Robbie reminded her. "We just came along for fun. Aren't you having fun?"

Beka didn't tell him how much she'd longed to work on one of her *own* Earth Pins this afternoon. Instead, she answered, "It's hard to have fun when you know something bad's going to happen."

"What do you mean?" Robbie asked. "How do you know something bad's going to happen?"

Callie raised a hand. "Guilty," she admitted. "I never return to Lake Park unless I'm needed. If something bad's going to happen, my job is to stay close — just in case."

Meanwhile, Crash was rummaging through her backpack. Pulling out a metal contraption, she carried it to the picnic table and began to set it up.

"Is dinner ready?" Rani called.

Crash gave her a frustrated look. "Almost," she answered. "I can still earn my pin by cooking on this."

The girls laughed.

"Ha," Callie said. "It's a backpacker stove."

"Paula," Mrs. Galt called. "Once the sun sets,

our light will disappear fast. Can we help you fix dinner so we don't have to eat in the dark?"

"But *I'm* the one working on the pin," Crash argued.

"You'll still get credit," the leader said. "It's up to you to tell everyone else what to do."

That brought a smile from Crash, making her braces glint in the sunset.

The sudden bustle of activity around the table brought Thatch to life. Thanks to all his "help," the girls had to don sweatshirts to ward off the ghost dog chill.

Crash was in high spirits, giving orders here and there. Rani built up the fire until it got to the "roaring" stage. Soon everyone gathered around the table for a dinner of red beans, rice, and carrot sticks.

Beka drew back from the giggling group. She couldn't share tonight's gaiety. Not when Callie's foreboding prediction hung over the campsite like a gray cloud.

Not knowing *what* was going to happen, or *who* it might happen to was unnerving.

With every dip of the setting sun, Beka's creepy feeling grew stronger.

How could Robbie and Callie sit there by the

fire, laughing and chatting, when something awful was bound to happen any minute?

Wandering further from the inviting warmth of the fire, Beka leaned against the smooth trunk of an aspen to be alone — and to ponder Callie's somber warning.

11
The Rajah's Story

Darkness arrived like the click of a light switch.

That's how it was in the mountains. One minute, twilight cast a golden glow across the hills to please you; the next, rocks and branches reached out in the dark to trip you.

The girls traded shorts for jeans, and topped sweatshirts with jackets.

"Are you okay?" Amber asked Mrs. Galt.

The leader had grown quiet. Beka had noticed it earlier, and even Robbie commented on it.

"I'm fine." Mrs. Galt seemed startled by the question. Removing the whistle from around her neck, she tossed it on top of the clipboard at her feet.

"Sorry, girls," she said with a sigh. "This spot always brings back memories of my own days as a MAC girl." A nostalgic look brushed her face. "Hey!" she exclaimed, changing the subject. "I think it's time for s'mores."

"Yea!" cheered the girls.

Mrs. Galt organized an assembly line.

Amber placed graham crackers on five squares of tin foil and passed them one by one to Rani.

Rani unwrapped chocolate bars and placed one on each cracker.

Leah topped the chocolate with marshmallows.

Crash placed another graham cracker on top, then sealed the foil around each s'more.

Mrs. Galt set the foil packets on the hot coals with a pair of tongs.

Soon, the insides melted into a gooey treat.

The leader served one to each girl on a paper plate.

Beka watched from the shadows. The scene made her smile — especially watching Thatch lick the sticky foil wrappings after the girls set them aside.

Suddenly Mrs. Galt sprang to her feet.

The girls stopped chatting to stare at her.

"I'm going for a little walk," she told them. Fumbling in her waist pack, she pulled out a tiny flashlight. "You girls enjoy yourselves. I'll be back in a few minutes."

"Are you sure ya'll are okay?" Leah asked.

Mrs. G. wiggled the flashlight like a Fourth-of-July sparkler to show them she was fine. "I'm really proud of each one of you, and all the hard work you did today. And I promise to attend your team's award ceremony to watch you receive your pins."

"Cool," said Amber.

Mrs. Galt gave them a quick wave. Stepping away from the circle, she disappeared into the dark forest.

"Are you ready?" Rani asked.

"For what?" asked the others.

"To hear the rest of the rajah's story."

Groans filled the air.

"*I'm* ready," Robbie said, nabbing Mrs. Galt's spot in the circle.

Callie looked confused as she sat close to the group. "Who's the rajah?"

Beka was eager to hear the end of the story. Sitting next to Callie, she quickly filled her in on the unfinished tale.

While Amber begged Rani to begin, Leah told her how silly the story was, and Crash asked her to talk about something less scary — even boys.

With all the distractions, no one noticed that the remaining graham crackers and marshmallows were quickly disappearing — thanks to Thatch.

Robbie caught him before the dog ripped into the chocolate bars. "Lie down, troublemaker," he told the ghost dog. "It's story time."

Rani held a flashlight under her chin. The beam cast a scary glow across her face. "When we left the rajah," she began in a quivery voice, "he'd just finished eating a lavish dinner in the great hall of the haunted palace."

"Stop," Crash said.

Everyone complained.

"I *meant* turn off the flashlight. You're giving me the creeps."

Rani clicked off the light. "Fine. It's better in the dark."

Crash groaned. "How come you didn't tell us last night that the palace was haunted?"

"I didn't?" Rani leaned into the firelight to give Crash an evil grin. "Well, it is."

"Eww-EEE-eww," Amber threw in.

"What happened next?" Leah asked.

Beka thought Leah was awfully interested in the ghost story she didn't want to hear.

"A storm blew in," Rani whispered. "Lightning and thunder shook the walls of the palace."

"It *always* lightnings and thunders in stories like this," Crash whimpered.

"O-o-o-o-o-o," Amber howled. "Ka-BOOM!"

The girls pelted her with gravel and twigs.

Amber ducked. "I'm just doing sound effects," she yelped.

"The wind snuffed the torchlights," Rani continued without missing a beat. "The only light left was a fire on the hearth. Suddenly, footsteps echoed in the dark palace. The rajah stood and drew his sword."

Rani paused for effect. "Then, an Indian princess appeared at the top of a spiral rock stairway. In the fire's glow, she was the most beautiful girl the rajah had ever seen.

" '*Put away your sword,*' she told him."

"No!" Crash cried. "Don't put it away!"

"Hu-ush." Leah smacked her on the arm.

" '*I am Princess Kamala. Stay, and we shall be wed. Then you will help me rule my kingdom.*' "

Amber wrinkled her nose. "Just like *that* she proposes marriage?"

Nervous giggles erupted around the fire.

" '*Why?*' the rajah asked. '*Why are you offering this to me?*' He wanted to say *yes*, but it all seemed too easy.

"The princess descended the spiral steps. '*I've*

been waiting for one I fancy to ride into my king-dom,' Princess Kamala told him. *'You are the first.'* She stepped into the glow of the fire so he could see just how beautiful she was. *'Do you accept?' "*

"No, no, no!" blurted Crash. "It's a trick!"

Amber yanked a cat bandanna from around her neck and playfully tried to stuff it into Crash's mouth.

Crash pushed it away. "Okay, okay," she said, but her voice was *not* light and playful.

Beka watched Crash's gaze circle the campsite.

Ha, she thought. *No one else is concerned that phantoms are lurking beyond their cozy fire circle. No one — except the girl with a sixth sense for ghosts.*

12
Squirrels Don't Eat Marshmallows

The other girls remained unaware of Crash's turmoil as Rani continued her story:

"The rajah bowed and took Princess Kamala's hand. At that moment, lightning flashed. In the split second of bright light, the beautiful princess became an ugly hag, dressed in rags, and bent with age."

"Gross," Amber said.

"The rajah stared at her, but now, all he could see was the beautiful young girl.

" '*Come*,' she said, taking his hand. '*My father, the king, will marry us. Then he will die, and everything in the kingdom shall be ours.*'

" '*Why must he die?*' the rajah asked.

" '*It is written in the old books*,' she told him. '*It is his fate.*'

"Suddenly, lightning flashed again. The rajah swore that the one who stood before him was a horrible, disgusting hag. But only for a second.

"As the rajah followed the princess up the spiral rock stairway, he heard his horse neigh.

" '*My horse!*' he cried. '*I've left my horse out in the storm. I must attend to him.*'

" '*NO!*' shrieked the princess. '*You must come with me. NOW. My servants will look after your horse.*'

" '*What servants?*' the rajah asked. He hadn't seen anyone else in the palace."

Beka glanced at Robbie. She'd been waiting for him to stage another haunting in the middle of Rani's scary tale. But his eyes (and ears) were glued to the storyteller.

Ha. Beka came to her feet. *Tonight's haunting is all up to me.* Her mind began to conjure up something scary she could do to frighten the girls.

A sudden rumble of thunder shook the ground beneath them.

The girls screamed.

Beka grinned and sat down. *That* was better than any kind of haunting *she* could come up with.

Leah bolted from the circle, then stopped, realizing she was safer in the fire's glow than any place else.

"Ah want more graham crackers," Leah said, settling back into her spot. "Scary stories make me hungry."

"Me, too," Amber added. "Toss me the marshmallows."

Rani lifted two empty packages from the ground.

The girls gaped at them.

"We had *lots* of graham crackers left over," Rani said. "I know we did. And marshmallows, too."

"Gulp!" Amber blurted, making everyone titter nervously.

"Here." Rani tossed a chocolate bar to each girl. "I guess the squirrels got the crackers and marshmallows."

"*I* didn't see any squirrels," Amber protested.

"Squirrels don't eat marshmallows," Crash mumbled.

Rani picked up the whistle and blew it.

The unexpected blast returned everyone's attention to her.

"May I *please* finish my story?"

"Hey, that's Mrs. G.'s whistle," Crash said. "Hasn't she been gone a long time?"

Thunder boomed again. Louder and closer.

The air grew heavy with the scent of rain.

"It's going to storm," Amber whispered. "Mrs. Galt told us she'd be gone only a few minutes."

"It's been at least a half hour," Leah added.

Crash leaped to her feet, peering into the darkness. "Do you think we need to look for her?"

The girls were quiet, pondering the question.

"She's *terrible* with directions," Rani reminded everybody. "What if she's lost and can't find her way back?"

"And she doesn't have her whistle to help us find her?"

"And it starts to rain?"

"And we're alone in the woods with a captive rajah and an evil hag pretending to be a princess?"

More nervous laughter.

Callie sprang to her feet as the girls' words sank in. "Mrs. Galt!" she cried. "I thought I was supposed to keep an eye on the MAC girls, but it's their *leader* who could be in danger — and I didn't even *think* of following her."

"Whoa," Beka said. "None of us did." She exchanged worried glances with her brother.

Moving quickly, Robbie stepped from the circle to watch and listen for movements in the trees.

Then Beka noticed Thatch. His ears were lifted, and he was sniffing the air the way he did whenever something was wrong.

The ghost dog began to bark. Then, with an urgency that surprised Beka, he bolted into the dark trees and disappeared.

13

Search Parties

Robbie chased after Thatch until he lost the dog in the darkness. When he returned to the firelight, worry creased his face.

"What should we do?" Beka asked.

"What should we do?" Crash cried at the same instant.

Beka hoped the girls didn't dash off into the middle-of-the-night forest. Keeping track of all of them would be impossible.

"We need a plan," Robbie answered.

"We need a plan," Amber said.

Beka turned to Callie to ask her opinion.

She was gone.

"Rob, where's Callie?"

Robbie pivoted, looking for her. "I guess she went after Mrs. Galt."

Beka was miffed. "She could've at least waited until we figured out what to do."

"*Thatch* didn't wait," Robbie told her. "Why should Callie? She's been trying to figure out her reason for being here. This might be it."

Beka had to agree. Still, Callie could have included them. After all, *they* were the resident ghosts of Kickingbird Lake.

Meanwhile, the MAC girls were scattering in all directions, hollering for their leader, and listening for distant replies — which never came.

"We need to organize a search party," Rani said. "Who has flashlights?"

All the girls dove for their backpacks, pulling out flashlights.

"Ah'm not traipsing through the forest in the dark," Leah said.

"Then you stay here," Rani told her. "Someone needs to remain at camp. Maybe you should find Mrs. G.'s first-aid kit, and have it ready, um, just in case."

"Plus," Amber added, "you'd better drag our sleeping bags and packs into the tent, or they'll get soaked."

Leah seemed relieved to be off the hook, but not interested in having chores to do.

"Should we stay together or spread out?" Amber asked.

"Stay together," Crash answered. Her voice was a nervous whisper.

"No," Rani objected. "We don't know which way Mrs. G. wandered. We need to split up to cover the most ground."

In the glow of the fire, Crash's freckles lined up in a worried frown. "What if *we* get lost?"

Rani sighed. "Just *don't*, okay?"

Beka hated how much time they were wasting while deciding what to do. "Raz, let's *go*."

"Don't you think we should follow the girls instead of looking for Mrs. Galt?"

"Why? *She's* the one who's missing."

"But Thatch and Callie have gone after her. She's in good hands. It's these others I'm not too sure about."

"Good point," Beka said. "I'll follow Crash. What about you?"

"Mmm. I don't think Rani needs anyone's help. I'll follow Amber."

"Good luck," Beka said, hurrying after the redhead, who was tiptoeing in the *opposite* direction Mrs. Galt had gone. "Maybe she thinks Mrs. G. got turned around and wandered the other way," Beka mumbled, trying to second-guess the girl.

Staying close to the glow of the flashlight was easy since Crash wasn't moving very fast. And her feeble cries of "Mrs. Galt, where are you?" were drowned out in the rumbling thunder.

Feeling helpless, Beka scouted ahead. She was used to "hinting" at people to go a certain direction. *Leading* Crash the right way would've been easier than following her meandering trail, yet Beka didn't *know* the right way any more than Crash did.

A sudden lightning flash and crack of thunder made Beka flinch, knocking her head against a low tree branch. "Ouch!" she cried.

Rubbing her head, she groaned. Saying "ouch" was nothing more than a natural reflex. "It didn't hurt," she muttered to herself. "You're a ghost, remember?"

If Robbie were here, he'd be quick to remind her — after he stopped laughing.

Crash trudged past. Another crack of thunder made both of them freeze.

The sky let loose, dumping torrents of rain so heavy, it seemed as though someone had turned on a giant faucet.

"Rats," Beka mumbled, scowling at the black sky. She hated rain and she hated loud noises. For two cents she'd head back to camp — with or without Crash.

"Mrs. G.!" Crash whisper-shouted. "Please answer!"

But no one did.

The girl moved on.

Rain rapidly turned the dirt beneath their feet into slippery mud.

Beka was having a hard time walking — and so was Crash, holding out both arms for balance.

Suddenly a small animal, rushing for cover, darted across their path.

Crash shrieked. Turning, she raced *through* Beka, slipping and sliding. Her wild motions threw erratic flashlight beams into the branches.

THUNK!

"Whoops!" Beka cringed, watching Crash reel from a blow to her forehead. She'd met the same low branch Beka had met earlier.

Beka couldn't believe she'd heard the *thunk* over the noisy rain. "Ouch . . . !" This time, she said the word in sympathy for the redhead, who was out cold, sprawled in the mud beneath the tree.

"Crimeny." Beka slumped against the trunk. "Now what?"

Should she wait for the girl to wake up? Or go for help?

"Crash is a good name for you," Beka told her.

Lightning and thunder struck again, making her uneasy.

Lying under a tree in an electrical storm wasn't the safest place to be.

Besides, what if Crash had bumped her head hard enough to need a doctor?

Waiting wasn't the right choice.

Beka sighed. Emergencies like this were much easier to handle when Robbie and Thatch were with her.

"I'll be right back," she whispered. "Don't go anywhere."

Beka picked her way through the dripping trees toward camp. Then she remembered. Robbie and Thatch weren't there.

Neither was Callie.

"I need help!" Beka shouted at the uncooperative sky. "Who's going to help me?"

The sky's unexpected answer was loud and abrupt, pushing Beka into a frantic run.

14
Lost and Found

L eah. She was the only one back at camp.
Leah was *not* Beka's first choice.

"*Thatch* is my first choice," Beka mumbled as she raced through the forest in the direction she *thought* was camp.

"Sorry, Rob," she added. "But Thatch knows how to rescue stranded MAC girls. It's his job."

She burst through heavy underbrush. A wall of jagged boulders rose in front of her. "This isn't the way we came."

Twirling, Beka squinted at her surroundings. Lightning flashes showed unfamiliar terrain.

"Great." She sighed in frustration. "I'm lost."

Beka batted at the raindrops. She wasn't wet.

The rain fell through her. Still, she sensed its coldness and wetness, and it wasn't very pleasant.

"How can I find my way in the dark?" She glared at the black clouds, still blotting out moonlight and stars — but it didn't make her feel any better.

Beka slowed to a slip-sliding walk. "We started out with one missing person, and now we have *two* missing persons and one missing *ghost.*"

Where was Thatch now that she needed him?

"Thatch!" she yelped, remembering the time he'd come to her when she'd called him in her mind. Should she try it now?

A bolt of lightning made her stop in her tracks. She froze, waiting for the *BOOM* that was bound to follow.

"Thatch!" she screamed, suddenly terrified at being alone in a noisy forest that seemed to be melting around her. "Hurry, puppy! I need you!"

After the thunder, Beka repeated the plea. Closing her eyes, she imagined Thatch tearing toward her through the rain-soaked trees.

Worries interrupted her concentration. Was it wrong to call him? What if he was hot on Mrs. Galt's trail right now? What if the other girls needed him?

Well, *Crash* needed the ghost dog, too. And so did she.

Puppy! her mind shouted. *You've got to find me!*

Beka's mind picture of Thatch racing toward her was so vivid, when she opened her eyes and saw the same scene, she thought she was imagining it.

"Woof!"

Beka knew she hadn't imagined his bark.

"Puppy!"

Thatch jumped up on her, licking her face, making sure she was all right. Beka had never been so happy to see the ghost dog. *And*, she was thankful mud didn't stick to his paws, or she'd be covered in dirty dog prints.

Hugging him, she ruffled his fur, amazed to find it completely dry in spite of the *gullywasher*, as her grandfather used to call summer rainstorms.

"I'm lost," she told Thatch, wondering if he already knew. "Now that you're here, maybe we should rescue Crash instead of going back to camp."

Thatch accepted the challenge. Minutes later, he found the girl, guiding Beka with his bark.

Beka was glad her dog was so good at finding

people. Tonight, she was having as much trouble figuring out directions as Mrs. Galt did.

Crash was sitting up, holding her head, shivering in the downpour.

Thatch tried to nudge her to her feet.

It worked.

Not because he actually did it, but because Crash suddenly sensed his presence, and jumped up.

"I've got to get out of here," she stammered, starting off in the direction they'd been hiking.

"Wait," Beka called. Even *she* knew Crash was going the wrong way. "Thatch, lead us back," Beka told him, then stopped. Thatch was smart, but he didn't know where "back" was. "Find Robbie," Beka commanded.

If Thatch led her to Robbie, at least the ghost trio would be together again — which would help her mood a whole lot. "Robbie needs you," Beka whispered into Thatch's ear. "Go get him."

The ghost dog lit out through the trees.

"Not so fast!" Beka hollered. "I have to get Crash turned around."

Thatch paused a few yards away and waited.

Beka circled ahead to block the girl's path. "Turn around, turn around, turn around," she chanted. "You're going the wrong way."

Crash didn't need much prompting. She stopped midstep, whipping her flashlight through the trees. "Hey, this isn't the way I came."

"Told ya so," Beka said, as Thatch barked. Was he in a hurry? Was more ghost work waiting to be done?

Crash turned and headed after Thatch.

Soon the rain let up, slowing to a trickle.

When they arrived at camp, no one was in sight.

Rain had doused the fire. The only light was a dim one, flickering inside Mrs. Galt's tent.

Crash ran to the tent and unzipped the door, kneeling to look inside.

Only one person was there. Leah. Cozy and dry. Reading a magazine by flashlight while snacking on pretzels.

"Yuck," she exclaimed at the sight of Crash. "Ya'll better not come in here wet and muddy."

"You mean, the others aren't back yet?" Crash's dirty face looked anxious.

Leah shook her head.

Beka suspected that Leah liked being alone in the tent, snug and warm.

Leah reached for a handful of pretzels. "Eww, what happened to ya'll's forehead?"

Crash gingerly touched her head, wiping away blood.

A whining noise drew Beka's attention.

Thatch still waited for her to follow.

"Whoops," she said. "I told you to find Robbie, and we haven't found him yet." Beka glanced at Crash and Leah. "Well, these two should be fine now, so let's — "

Crash came to her feet, tilting her head to listen to the *drip, drip, drip* of leftover raindrops falling from leaves.

"What are you doing?" Leah called.

"I'm going to keep looking for Mrs. G.," Crash said. "For some strange reason, I think she's that-away." She pointed straight at Thatch.

"Your 'some strange reason' is a ghost dog who's trying to lead you to Robbie — except you don't know who Robbie is."

"Are you coming?" Crash asked, peering into the tent.

Leah made a face. "Rani told me to stay here, so I will."

"Good excuse," the redhead said. A hint of sarcasm touched her voice. "You're the only dry one. Might as well stay put."

"Ta-tah, then!" Leah snuggled into her sleeping bag and tore into a bag of Fritos. "Zip me in?" she asked.

Crash zipped the tent closed, then hurried after

Thatch. Only she didn't *know* she was following a ghost dog.

Anxiety pushed Beka quickly along after her. Where was Thatch taking them?

Was Mrs. Galt all right?

Or was bad news waiting somewhere over the next dark hill . . . ?

15

Midnight Conversation
With a Ghost

Now that the rain has stopped, the night is rather pleasant, Beka thought. Everything smelled fresh and new. Stars peeked through breaks in clouds, and even the edge of the moon, knife-blade thin, was visible.

In the uneven light, the direction Thatch was leading them seemed familiar.

Beka tried to get her bearings, but Crash was swirling the flashlight as she walked, making it difficult to see much.

Soon they came to the top of a rise, ending in a cliff, which dropped off to a wooded area. Below was the former site of the MAC girl cabin — long since burned to the ground.

Whispered voices drew Crash and Beka to the

edge of the cliff. Amber, Rani, and Robbie were leaning over a rock, peering at the scene below.

Beka hurried to see what held them so spellbound.

Thatch loped toward Robbie, breaking his concentration. "Hey, you guys are here!" he exclaimed. "Good. Come take a look at this."

Beka and Crash leaned over the boulder at the same time.

Below, barely visible in the meager light, a tall figure sat on the cement wall of the cabin's foundation.

"Is it Mrs. Galt?" Beka whispered, then wondered why she was whispering.

"That's what the girls are trying to decide." Robbie motioned toward Rani and Amber. "But it *is* her. I've been down there. Callie was talking to Mrs. G., so I left them alone."

"Talking to Mrs. G.?" Beka echoed. "You mean they were actually *talking* to each other?"

"Yes — but Mrs. G. didn't know it."

"Huh?"

Robbie grabbed Thatch's collar to keep him from dashing down the hill. "Hold up a minute, boy; she doesn't need your help right now."

Beka elbowed her brother in the ribs. "Don't leave me in suspense."

"Sorry. How can I explain it? Mrs. G. was talking out loud. Callie was answering back, only Mrs. G. didn't hear Callie or know she was there."

"Oh." Although confusing, Beka understood. "But Mrs. G. got Callie's message, right? Like, when we have 'conversations' with people, they can't hear us, but they get the hint."

"I think so." Robbie tried to distract Thatch, whose eyes were glued on the figure below. "Mrs. G. started crying. Callie sat and talked to her for a long, long time."

"Where's Callie now?" Beka moved to get a better view, but she couldn't find the other ghost.

"I don't know. She sort of disappeared when I wasn't paying attention."

The girls' voices made Beka stop and listen.

"It *is* Mrs. G.," Rani insisted. "Now that the moon's coming out, it's easy to tell who it is."

"Okay," Amber agreed. "I just didn't want to go barging down there if it was somebody else. Especially since it sounded like she was crying."

"Let's go," Rani urged. "She might need our help."

The girls clicked on their flashlights, and found a place to scale down the rise. Crash descended the hill mostly on her bottom.

The twins found a quicker route, but not as quick as Thatch, who was at Mrs. Galt's side seconds after Robbie let go of his collar.

"Oh, my!" the leader exclaimed as she saw the army of MAC girls stumbling toward her in the dark.

Coming off the cement wall, she placed both hands over her heart. "When I saw the flashlight beams, it scared me. I thought you were prowlers, and here I'd left my charges up at the campsite all alone."

The instant the girls reached her, Mrs. Galt swept them all into a hug.

"Are you all right?"

"We thought you were lost."

"You scared us."

"Why didn't you come back?"

The questions tumbled out faster than the leader could answer them. "Sit down a minute, and I'll tell you what happened."

The girls found places to sit on an L-shaped section of the cabin's foundation.

Beka circled behind the cement wall. "Callie?" she hollered. "Where are you?"

Robbie made a wide sweep of the area, helping Beka search. "She's gone," he finally said.

"Why would she leave?"

"She came here to do her job. Maybe she finished, and had no reason to stay any longer."

"Well, she could've at least said good-bye."

Beka felt offended. She liked Callie, and hoped they could be friends. "So what was her *job?*"

"Talking to Mrs. Galt?"

His answer was a question, meaning, Beka assumed, he didn't really know.

"Callie said she came back when people needed help *one way or another*." Robbie paused to inspect the remains of the fireplace. "Besides, I think they knew each other. Why else would Mrs. G. call Callie by name?"

"She *did?*" Beka grabbed his arm. "She called Callie by *name?*"

"Yeah. Didn't I mention that?"

"No!"

"Whoops." Robbie motioned toward the group sitting on the wall. "Maybe we'd better listen in on Mrs. G.'s explanation."

Beka didn't need a second invitation. In three steps, she was back with the group, hoping her search for Callie hadn't made them miss the leader's story about her midnight conversation with a ghost.

16
Ghost Bumps

Robbie and Beka found a good sitting spot on an adjoining wall.

Thatch was already settled into a bed of damp leaves, gazing up at Mrs. G. as though he wanted to hear the story, too.

The girls were jabbering away, telling the leader how they'd launched search parties, why Leah hadn't come with them, and why Crash's forehead was cut and swollen.

Mrs. Galt peered at the stars as if they held some great secret. "Girls, I'm really sorry I upset you. I guess I owe you an explanation for my strange behavior."

Sighing, she began. "When I told you I was going for a short walk, I'd *meant* to do exactly that. I wanted to see if I could find this cabin — or the spot where it used to be."

Pausing, she gestured at the cabin's crumbling walls. "I didn't expect to find the foundation still here. Seeing it shook me up a little."

The same look of nostalgia Beka had noticed earlier swept across the leader's face.

"The summer I was ten," Mrs. G. began, "my best friend and I came to Lake Park for a retreat. It was our reward for earning more Earth Pins than anyone else in our troop."

"Rob!" Beka rasped, making the connection. "I'll bet Callie was her best friend, which means she's — "

"Debby," Robbie finished for her.

"Whoa," Beka whispered. "She's a grown-up, and Callie is still only ten. . . ."

Mrs. Galt glanced at her audience. "I belonged to the MAC girl Moose Team. We had a wonderful time here, Callie and me, until the last night.

"A summer thunderstorm moved in, much like the one we had tonight — quite unexpected, which is the way it happens in the mountains. Lightning struck a tree near the cabin. Minutes later, a burning branch fell onto the roof and set the cabin on fire.

"All the lights went out. I'll never forget how dark it was. I had trouble finding my way out."

99

Stopping, she gave them a sheepish look. "You might have noticed I have a little trouble with directions."

The girls laughed, but it was a polite laugh, Beka thought.

"Between the rain and the hail — and the other girls' screams — it was impossible to hear what the leaders were telling us to do.

"I couldn't find Callie, then all of a sudden she was there — dripping wet. She'd gotten out safely, then come back for me. If she hadn't, well, I'm not sure I would have made it; I was so scared. Between the darkness and smoke, I was completely turned around, and couldn't even find the stairs."

"Why didn't you and Callie run outside together?" Amber asked in a quiet voice.

"Callie tried. She grabbed my hand, but I let go and ran back to our room to save the necklace I'd just gotten for my birthday."

The leader touched her neck as if feeling for the long-lost locket. "It had my initials on it," she added. "D.A.W. My maiden name was Ward."

"Yikes," Beka whispered. "This is so weird."

"I thought it would only take a second to grab my necklace, and it did. Still," Mrs. G. added, "seconds *count* in a burning cabin."

"But Callie came back for you," Rani said, urging her on.

"Yes. She led me out through an open window. Everything would have been fine, except I dropped the necklace as I was climbing outside. Callie went back to get it, and . . ." Mrs. Galt stopped. "Gosh, this happened so long ago — thirty-some years. Yet, it's as clear in my mind as if it happened yesterday."

"Callie didn't get out in time, did she?" Rani whispered.

Mrs. Galt shook her head.

The girls were quiet for a few moments.

"Hearing the same story from both points of view is spooky," Robbie muttered.

"No kidding." Beka rubbed her arms. "The story is giving me goose bumps."

"Me, too," Robbie said. "Only mine are *ghost bumps*."

Beka groaned.

"We're sorry, Mrs. Galt," Crash said.

Smiling, the leader patted Crash on the leg. "The oddest thing happened tonight as I was sitting here by myself. I've never forgotten Callie, of course. I've always felt responsible for her, even though I *begged* her not to go back.

"Sitting here, remembering that night, I suddenly felt as if Callie were right here beside me."

"She was," Beka whispered.

"I felt as if she told me not to worry about it anymore, and that she didn't blame me. It's like I've been carrying one of these cement blocks around on my shoulders for thirty years, and now it's been lifted away."

"Cool," Amber said, then felt embarrassed, as if that wasn't the proper thing to say.

But it made Mrs. Galt laugh. "Yes, it *is* cool. And I feel great now. The end of an unfinished chapter in my life has finally been written."

She hopped off the cement wall. "Thank you, girls, for letting me share my story with you."

The twins waited while everybody hugged everybody else.

Meanwhile, *they* hugged Thatch, who was acting so mellow and content, Beka wondered if he understood why Callie had come and gone.

"Everybody back to camp," Mrs. G. ordered. "I could eat another s'more or three."

"Did you hear that, puppy?" Beka shook a finger at the guilty ghost dog. "Aren't you ashamed of yourself for eating all the s'more fixin's?"

Thatch looked her squarely in the eye.

"I think that means '*No, it was worth it,*' " Robbie interpreted.

Rani circled an arm around Mrs. Galt's waist.

"We will personally escort you back to camp to make *sure* you go the right direction."

The girls laughed.

Amber put her arm around Mrs. G.'s shoulders. "And about those s'mores," she began. "We have some *really* bad news. . . ."

17

The Sardine Sleepover

"**M**ove over," Leah snapped.

"There's no *room* to move," Amber shot back.

Thanks to the soggy ground, the girls were bedded down inside Mrs. Galt's "three-person tent" — making it more like a "five-person sardine can."

Robbie had tried to convince Beka to spend what was left of the night with him and Thatch on the benches of the picnic table.

But she'd insisted on joining the MAC girls for their cramped sleepover, sprawling sideways across three sleeping bags.

"Why are you in such a bad mood?" Rani asked

Leah. "You got to stay inside tonight, warm and dry. *We* should be grumpy, not you."

"Hmmph," Leah answered. "Ah'm grumpy because Ah found one of ya'll's notebooks while cleaning up the campground, and Ah read what you wrote about me."

"Whoops!" Beka's heart skittered.

"Who's gonna admit it?" Leah muttered. "It said stuff about ya'll, too."

Crash adjusted the bandage on her forehead. "Was it *bad* stuff?"

"Oh, geez," Beka groaned.

"No, not bad. But I *don't* like being called *Prissy.*"

The other girls snickered.

"Don't laugh," Leah snipped.

"Girls," came Mrs. G's. voice. "Fess up. Who owns the notebook?"

Silence filled the darkness inside the tent.

"What did it say about *me?*" Amber asked, her voice full of curiosity.

"It said you were *Fuh-ney.*"

"Oh, thank you." Now Amber sounded pleased.

"It said Rani was *Cool,* and Crash was *Confused,*" Leah finished.

"Mmm," came Mrs. Galt's voice. "Sounds like the notebook belongs to someone *outside* this group." She clicked on her flashlight. "Show it to me."

Leah fumbled in the dim light. "Hey, it's gone!"

Beka clasped the notebook to her chest. "Ta-tah!" She gave Leah a victory grin. "Didn't think I'd let you *keep* it, did you?"

Leah struggled out of her sleeping bag to search. "It was right here beside mah sleeping bag."

"I didn't take it," Amber blurted.

"Neither did I," added Rani.

In the beam of the flashlight, Crash's eyeballs were about to pop out of her head.

A strange expression shadowed Mrs. Galt's face. She clicked off the light. "Go to sleep, girls," she whispered.

"But — " Leah protested.

"Sometimes things happen that can't be explained," Mrs. G. said.

"You're telling *me*," Crash mumbled.

One minute of quiet passed.

"Rani?" Amber whispered in the dark.

"Mmm?"

"Finish the rajah's story."

The girls mumble-groaned.

"I'm too sleepy."

"Please?" Amber jabbed at Rani's sleeping bag.

"Okay, okay." Rani yawned loudly. "The rajah

took Princess Kamala to the doctor and got her some anti-hag pills to cure her, then they went to the mall and picked out her wedding dress. The king married them, and didn't die, like the old books said he would, and the rajah and the princess lived happily ever after."

"BOOOOOO! HISSSSSSS! BOOOOOO!"

"Well, it's a very *modern* fairy tale."

And those were the last words the MAC girls could get out of Rani.

18
One More Earth Pin

At the bottom of the trail, the MAC girls hurried through Lake Park, off toward the souvenir shops Mrs. Galt had promised them.

Robbie and Beka stayed behind to wander through the garden maze, and wait for Thatch, who'd disappeared.

"Where *is* he?" Beka asked after finding her way through the tangly maze five times.

"Woof!" came a distant bark.

"There he is!" Robbie pointed toward the cemetery. "Here, boy."

Thatch wouldn't come.

"Maybe he's cornered a cat. Let's go see."

Thatch waited for them to find him. Sitting on

a walkway, he wagged his tail as if he'd just performed a string of tricks.

"Come on," Beka urged. "If we miss the Kickingbird ferry, it's a lo-o-o-o-ong walk home."

Thatch wouldn't budge.

"What's wrong, puppy?" Beka let her gaze wander the area.

The grave marker next to Thatch caught her eye. She moved closer. "Raz!" Beka gasped. "Look!"

Thatch wiggled around as though he was pleased with Beka's find.

"Callie Maria Lopez," Robbie read.

"Look at the dates," Beka added. "Nineteen fifty to nineteen sixty. Ten years."

"Her kindness and helpfulness will always be remembered," Robbie said, reading the rest of the headstone.

"And she's *still* being kind and helpful," Beka added, liking the idea the more she thought of it.

"What's this?" Robbie reached for something in the grass.

"Woof!"

"Whatever it is, Thatch wanted us to find it." Beka watched Robbie brush away grass and leaves.

"It's an Earth Pin!" Beka yelped, snatching it

away from her brother. "Look, it shows the emblem of a *ghost* — ha!"

Robbie shook his head in amazement. "So Callie *did* say good-bye — by awarding you the Ghost Pin you spent the weekend earning."

BLEEEEEEP!

"It's the warning whistle from the ferry!" Robbie ran for the gate. "We've only got three minutes to get onboard."

Thatch zoomed ahead. His "mission" in the cemetery had been accomplished.

Beka started to run, then paused for one brief message to Callie:

"Thank you for the pin," she whispered. *"I hope I get to see you again."*

Then she bolted after Robbie and Thatch, knowing Callie had *somehow* gotten her ghostly message.

Rules to Ghost by

1. Ghosts can touch objects, but not people or animals. Ghost hands go right through them.
2. Ghosts can cause a "disturbance" around people to get their attention. Here are four ways: a) walk through them; b) yell and scream; c) chant a message; d) stand close enough to give them a *ghost chill*.
3. Ghost rules aren't always logical — rules of the world don't apply to ghosts.
4. Thatch's ghost-dog powers are stronger than ours. He can do things we can't. Sometimes he even teaches us things we didn't know we could do.
5. Ghosts can't move through closed doors, walls, or windows (but we can *smoosh* through if there is even one tiny hole).

6. Ghosts don't need to eat, but can if they want to.
7. Ghosts can listen in on other people's conversations.
8. Ghosts can move objects by concentrating until they move into "our ghost world" and become invisible. When we let go, the object becomes visible again.
9. Ghosts don't need to sleep, but can rest by "floating." If our energy is drained (by too much haunting or *smooshing*) we must return to Kickingbird Lake to renew our strength.
10. Ghosts can move from one place to another by thinking hard about where they want to go, and wishing it. It only works when Thatch helps us.

New Rules!

11. We can make people see us if we try hard to "think solid." It really *scares* people — but that's what ghosts are supposed to do!
12. The Ghost Leap: Helps us jump over tall bushes, wide streams, and huge rocks that are more than twice our height. Lets us move very quickly through forests and backyards.

Don't Miss!
The Mystery at Hanover School —
Ghost Twins #7

Robbie climbed over the "Do Not Enter" sign
and disappeared up the dark passageway inside
the bell tower.

Barking echoed from above, as if Thatch had
found something important.

Taking a deep breath, Beka scrambled over the
rope and tiptoed up the spiral steps. The air inside
the brick tower was cool and musty. Putting both
hands against the rough walls, she felt her way,
counting steps as she climbed — like she used to
fifty years ago. Then, there'd been twenty-two.

Beka stumbled in the dark, but as she neared
the top, an eerie light helped her see the crumbling steps.

The twisting passageway ended at an ill-fitting
door. Strange light seeped around its edges, cast-
ing foreboding rays across the rounded walls.

Thatch hunched at the top, sniffing like crazy
at the door.

Robbie turned to watch Beka come around the corner, climbing the last few steps. Uncertainty shadowed his face.

"Twenty-two, it is," she mumbled, unable to take her eyes off the door. Black metal hinges, shaped like rattlesnake fangs, held it in place.

"If I wasn't a ghost," Beka whispered, "I'd be flying down these steps, and as far from here as I could get."

About the Author

Dian Curtis Regan is the author of many books for young readers, including *Home for the Howlidays* and *My Zombie Valentine*. Ms. Regan graduated from the University of Colorado in Boulder. Presently, she lives in Edmond, Oklahoma, where she shares an office with her cat, Poco, seventy-six walruses, and a growing collection of "Thatch dogs."